WHITE WATER

by Jonathan and Aaron London · illustrated by Jill Kastner

VIKING

VIKING
Published by the Penguin Group
Penguin Putnam Books for Young Readers, 345 Hudson Street, New York, New York 10014, U.S.A.

Penguin Books Ltd, Registered Offices: Harmondsworth, Middlesex, England

First published in 2001 by Viking, a division of Penguin Putnam Books for Young Readers.

10 9 8 7 6 5 4 3 2 1

ISBN: 0-670-89286-6
Library of Congress cataloging-in-publication data is available.

Printed in Hong Kong   Set in Cheltenham   Book design by Teresa Kietlinski

The artwork was created using oil on paper.

For Roger, Lisa, Rowan, Dennis, and Skip
and the whole Mountain White Water gang
—J.L.

For the boys, Bryan, Jamey, and Will
—J.K.

Two hours by air, then four on the road,
and we were at the put-in on the Green River, in
Desolation Canyon, Utah, in the tumbleweed desert,
where we made camp for the night.

Dad told me again how much fun
white water rafting was.
"And by the end," he said,
"you'll learn to read the river—
which way looks safer,
which way is more dangerous."
I was quiet, thinking about how scary it
would be. Here the river was flat, but what
did it become around those huge rock walls?

Coyotes on the canyon rim woke us early—
or was it Wild Man Dennis yowling, "Come 'n' get it!"
We crawled out of our tents into a great feast of pancakes, hash browns,
and bacon. Dennis would be the cook for ten people for the next seven days.

As the sun climbed the mountains and filled the canyon with warmth,
we all chipped in, breaking camp, pumping air into the rafts,
loading them up, and strapping things down—otherwise things
would fly out when we hit the rapids, Dad said.
"What about us?" I wondered, as we pushed off.

But not all of river rafting is rapids. We rowed—Dad took turns
with Dennis and Roger—and we floated and got hotter
and pointed at eagles soaring overhead
and floated some more.

Then we heard it.
"Listen," said Dad.
"What's that?" I asked.
"*White water!*" he shouted.
We were moving faster. Roger was rowing.
The river seemed to suck us along. Roger
swung the raft around to face the rapids.
"Hang on tight!" Dad said.

All of a sudden the water was white,
as if thousands of white rabbits were jumping
around us. I clenched my teeth and fists as we
whipped and spun and bounced on waves.
"*Yee-ha!*" I yelled—and almost fell over backwards—
"*whups!*" and hung on.
That rapid was my first one, and it sure was fun.

We were starting to look for a place to
camp when another cry went up.
"Horses! Look at those horses!"
There on the steep bank stood four wild
horses and two colts. You could see their
muscles bulging as they grazed.
Suddenly the leader took off running,
and the rest followed, hooves pounding,
rocks sliding, the little colts racing behind.

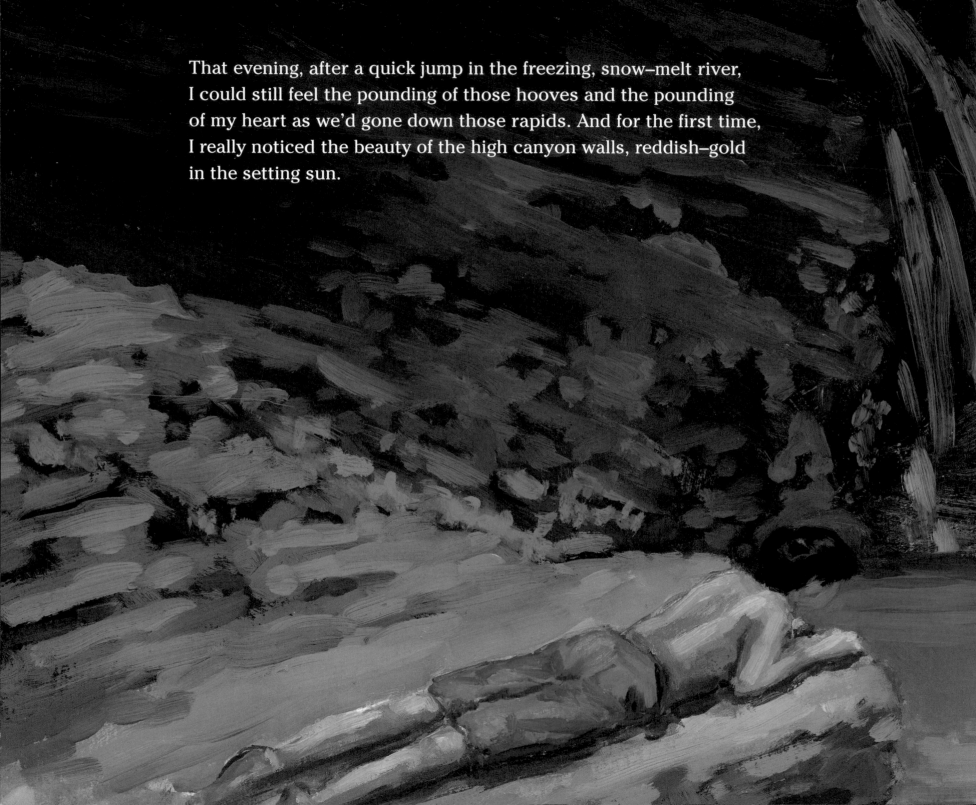

That evening, after a quick jump in the freezing, snow–melt river,
I could still feel the pounding of those hooves and the pounding
of my heart as we'd gone down those rapids. And for the first time,
I really noticed the beauty of the high canyon walls, reddish–gold
in the setting sun.

Over the next five river days we crashed through rapids, sat around the fire, ate great food, and slept under a billion bright stars. On our second-to-last day—in a smooth stretch of river—I was sitting at the oars opposite Dad, pushing when he pulled, and we were singing,
"Row, row, row your boat, *crashing* down the stream . . . "
when we heard the roar. It was the loudest yet, and it was getting closer.
"White water!" I hollered.

The first thing we hit was a huge hole like
a waterfall, followed by a wave as big
as a small house—
and we went flying. Dad's hat flew off.
We fell laughing and conked heads in the
bottom of the raft, but Roger Dodger
grabbed the oars and we made it through.

But it wasn't over yet. We smashed through four more rapids before we came to Rattlesnake Rapid. I tried to "read the river." At least two dozen boulders jutted out of the water, among haystack waves and deep holes. Some are called "keeper holes"—you get sucked in and never come out. I pointed at the smooth V in the current and shouted, "There's the tongue!"

Then it seemed the river swallowed us. Roger yelled, "*Bail!* Bail!"
We bailed hard, but our raft whipped and slammed against a rock
and got stuck—on the edge of a hole.
"High side! High side!" Roger shouted, and we all clung to the high side
of the raft to keep from flipping over. Lisa in the next raft threw us a line,
but the current was so fast, she missed. The last raft rolled by, and they
missed, too. The river was tumbling in. The hole was pulling us, pulling us.

Roger gripped the oars.
Dad and I helped. And together
we pulled so hard on those oars,
we thought they would break.
Instead, our raft was spit out
of the whirling hole . . .
and we were free.

That night—
our last on the river—
Wild Man Dennis roasted a
ten-pound slab of New York steak
and a dozen potatoes.
We sat around the fire and
Roger Dodger lifted a cup
and made a toast:
"To the river!"
"To the river!"

The river rats
all clinked cups, and Dad said,
"The river stole my hat,
and my heart."
And I said,
"Let's eat!"
And that was the best meal
I ever had and probably
ever will have.

I had learned to read the river,
and I liked what I read.